Praise for _Wrath_ by Mar

"Thought-provoking and atmospheric" *THE BOOKSELLER*

"A brilliantly unsettling novel that readers will race through" SARAH CROSSAN

"Meaningful, powerful, wonderful" TOM PALMER

"Such a delicately wrought and cleverly done piece of climate fiction, told through the lens of teenagers' lives. Really beautiful" LAUREN JAMES

"So, so good. A treasure. Exactly as brilliant as I thought it would be" DAN SMITH

"A thrilling, thought-provoking, timely novella ... _Wrath_ presents a poignantly original way of thinking about climate change and how we relate to each other" LOVEREADING4SCHOOLS

"Fast paced and engaging" *INIS*

"A multi-layered story with lots to engage teenage readers ... A powerful and thought-provoking mystery drama from a skilful storyteller, with a satisfying and hopeful ending too" *BOOKS FOR KEEPS*

"A fascinating and layered drama for all of Sedgwick's many fans" **THE BOOKBAG**

"Sedgwick is such a skilful writer and tells such a compelling story that it's hard to imagine that anyone picking this up could put it down until it's finished ... A real treat" **THE LETTERPRESS PROJECT**

"A layered, unsettling and intelligent novella that I'll be thinking about for a while" **ANNE THOMPSON, "A LIBRARY LADY"**

"What a wondrous little book; as bleak, yet beautiful and hopeful as the turning point in our planet's history at which we now find ourselves" **JAMES HADDELL**

"Literally no word is wasted ... I was completely enthralled" **PRIMARY TEACHER BOOKSHELF**

"A brilliant novella. Read in one sitting. Timely, intense, full of suspense" **JO BOWERS**

RAVENCAVE

MARCUS SEDGWICK

Barrington Stoke

First published in 2023 in Great Britain by
Barrington Stoke Ltd
18 Walker Street, Edinburgh, EH3 7LP

www.barringtonstoke.co.uk

A CIP catalogue record for this book is available
from the British Library upon request

ISBN: 978-1-80090-192-6

Printed by Hussar Books, Poland

For our ancestors

ONE

"This place is full of ghosts," says Mum. "This entire landscape."

No one answers her. They're walking ahead of me anyway – Mum, Dad, Robbie. I only hear Mum's voice because the wind picks it up and brings it down the path to me. I've stopped by the ruin – the ruin of Crackpot Hall.

The abandoned, derelict buildings stand over the wide valley below, but I don't see any ghosts. I don't see anyone at all – not a thing moving, not a person, not even a bird in the sky.

I've stopped because I can't go on. This often happens – my family have left me behind. They forget I can't keep up. Robbie is two years older than me, nearly three, in fact. And Mum and Dad are the types who march over mountains without a moment's thought.

They move on. I watch them go, leaving me further behind. I know we have to hurry. Dad explained that when we set out this morning.

"There's bad weather coming in later," he said. "I know it looks nice now, but we have to be back before mid-afternoon."

"We'll be fine," Mum replied, and Robbie said nothing. And then we set out later than we meant to. Which means no one is waiting for me. And I know we have to hurry. I know we do, because we came here to do this important thing for Dad. For his mum.

We leave tomorrow, after our week's holiday, and the weather hasn't been great. There hasn't been the chance to get up here. We've just been stuck in our rooms in the pub or visiting places. Mum and Dad have been getting cross with each other. It's rained a lot – not like last year, when it was sunny the whole time. That was the first time we came here, a year ago, around Easter too.

*

On that last visit, it was really hot, like summer. And one day we did the same walk as today, up past Crackpot Hall and beyond.

2

Exactly the same thing happened then. I remember stopping on this very same spot on this very same bend in the footpath. After this, the bend climbs up to the Hall and then snakes around the back of it, before running on, flatter again, to the east.

I stood here then, almost exactly a year ago, out of breath, while the others had gone ahead of me. I remember looking at the view of the valley, basking in hot spring sunshine. It felt too hot for the time of year. This seemed to be a place that was normally wet and grey and windy. But that day it was really hot. I wanted to go and swim in the waterfalls to cool off, but Mum and Dad wanted to walk, so that was what we did.

I stood and panted and looked down the valley, and I tried to connect with it. I tried to feel something for it. I tried to feel *anything*, just to please Dad, because that was mostly why we were here, that time a year ago. It was why we'd chosen the Yorkshire Dales for our holiday, so that Dad could poke around the villages where his grandparents and great-grandparents had lived. It had become so important to him, for some reason. He seemed to be upset that I felt nothing for the place, and neither did Mum or Robbie.

Dad would look at Robbie and me and say, "My grandfather was born here," or, "My great-grandmother was born there." We'd stand looking blankly at Dad, and he'd say, "They're your ancestors too, you know!" And still we'd look blankly at him, and he'd go quiet for hours.

Dad never used to be interested in his family history. Mum said it was his age – suddenly he wanted a sense of where he came from, or something.

Maybe she was right – that if Dad knows where he came from, he will know who he is. Whatever the reason, he's been obsessed with his family history now for a couple of years.

I also remember, a year ago, how I stopped just short of the Hall. Robbie came bounding back down the path to get me, full of excitement.

"You have to see this place!" Robbie said. "You won't guess what it's called."

So I made myself move again and followed Robbie into the ruin, panting in the heat.

The name Crackpot Hall makes it sound like it's some huge stately home, but it isn't that kind of place. It's a farmhouse, that's all. Or it was. It must have been one or maybe two large buildings with some outbuildings attached. But the roofs have all gone now, fallen in.

It's still a great place to play in, but Mum shouted at Robbie and me as we started climbing over walls, saying it wasn't safe. She said one day one of us would have a proper accident and then we'd learn to be more careful. Mum was probably right, but we ignored her for a bit until she got really cross, and then she went to go and look at the view.

Dad smiled at Robbie and me.

"Some spot, eh?" Dad said.

He stood looking down the valley. He'd forgotten the open guidebook in his hand. The landscape was ... I don't know how to describe it. Wide, open, green. Beautiful.

Sad too, somehow. I don't know why I thought that – I just felt it.

"They might have only been farmers who lived here," Dad added, "but they had a view fit for a king."

"Why do kings get the best of everything?" asked Robbie. But before anyone could answer, he ran off. Never stays still for long, does Robbie.

Dad stuck his nose back in the guidebook.

"Ha," he said. "Crackpot doesn't mean what you think it means."

"What do I think it means?" I asked.

"You think it means like a crazy person. A lunatic, right?"

"Maybe," I said, because that's exactly what I had been thinking.

Mum was coming back and heard.

"Crackpot means 'cave of the ravens'," she said.

Dad scowled at her, but in a funny way.

"How did you know that?" Dad asked.

"Read about it over breakfast," Mum said. She looked at me and explained, "Crackpot comes from old words. Norse words. The language that the Vikings spoke. Crack comes from their word for raven, *kraka*, and *pot* meant a cave or a hole. Actually, we still use that word. As in 'potholing' – when people go caving. So its real name is Ravencave."

"But I don't see any caves marked on the map," said Dad. "That's strange."

Mum shivered.

"Why anyone would want to crawl around in holes deep underground is beyond me," she said. "Some people do weird things for pleasure, don't they? Why go underground when you could be looking at all this beauty?"

She waved an arm at the view, but I wasn't seeing what Mum was seeing.

"There were Vikings here?" I asked. It was hard to believe anyone had ever been here, aside from walkers like us. Only the ruins of the farm showed that at some point people had lived here, high up, but I couldn't imagine what they'd been doing.

"Vikings?" Dad said. "Yes, they were here. A thousand years ago last Wednesday. "Give or take."

He chuckled and we set off again, leaving Crackpot Hall behind us.

That was all a year ago. And some things are the same and some things have changed.

Robbie is Robbie, but he is a new version of Robbie, one who doesn't seem to like me any more.

Meanwhile, I have a large scar on my knee from where I fell a year ago. I'd been trying to keep up with him, clambering over the rocks at the river fairly near here.

Mum was a writer, but she wasn't writing anything back then and she isn't now. In fact, I only have a vague memory of when she did write. Are you still a writer if you no longer write anything?

Dad tells Mum she still is a writer. He tells her all the time. It doesn't seem to help. In fact, it seems to make things worse. Mum was pretty successful once.

And then there's Dad. Things have changed for him because he lost his job – just a week before we came away. No one knows what's going to happen now. Mum's been working part-time at the local arts centre for about a year, but without Dad's income, things aren't looking good ...

I was amazed we still came on holiday this year, but Dad said, "It's all paid for already. We're going. And when we get back, I'll figure out what to do."

So we came, and here we are, four souls spread across the Yorkshire landscape. I am left wondering how it is that people go on. How do people keep on going, even when everything seems to be against them?

I watch Mum and Dad, twenty metres apart, higher up on the trail. Robbie is nowhere to be seen. He's already out of sight ahead of them, over the crest of the hill.

What makes people go on? I think.

Then I think, *I am too young to be thinking thoughts like this, aren't I?*

Then I decide that thought is weird in itself. I realise what's more important: I had better try to catch up before they lose me entirely.

I skirt around and above the back of the ruin of the place that should be called Ravencave Hall.

As I walk, I realise that I do know what makes Mum go on.

She's chasing ghosts.

People say that sometimes. They say, "Oh, so-and-so, he's chasing a ghost." It means they're doing something hopeless, looking for something that they will never find. But with Mum, it's different. She really is looking for ghosts, and this is not some silly pipe dream, because she has chased them before. And found them. Often.

TWO

Let me tell you this story, if you don't believe my mum can see ghosts, or if you don't believe in ghosts at all. I promise you it's true. I wasn't born at the time, nor Robbie. It happened when Mum and Dad were young – before they were married in fact.

They'd been seeing each other for a few months, and the time came for Mum to meet Dad's mum, my granny. Granny is the reason we've come back to the Yorkshire Dales this year. It's her ashes that we're going to spread, high up in Swaledale.

It's been a pretty difficult time recently. Granny died just a few weeks before Dad lost his job. In Granny's will, she said she wanted to go home. That meant, Dad explained, that she wanted her ashes spread where she was born, more or less. And that meant Swaledale. But that's not the story I'm telling now.

Granny moved to the South when she was just a kid, and married Dad's dad. They lived almost all their lives in an old cottage in Sussex. Granny stayed there after she became a widow. Not long after they started going out, Dad took Mum down there to stay one weekend.

Mum and Granny got on well right from the start. That evening, they all had tea in the old, low-beamed dining room. Later, Mum and Dad went to bed and were alone in their room, and Mum said, "Who was the old man in a black suit, sitting by the fireplace?"

Of course, there had been no one there, not a real person, not someone that anyone else could see. Only Mum saw the man in the black suit. She told Dad he should know this thing about her – that sometimes Mum sees stuff. Ghosts and "other things".

I used to ask her what she meant by "other things". But she said I was too young to be told, and she would always change the subject. I guessed that what she saw were dark things.

Scary things. Somehow it's worse not knowing exactly.

Anyway, Dad didn't believe Mum. He just went along with it. He didn't say she was lying, but he didn't actually believe her. And Dad didn't mention it to Granny, because he didn't want to scare her, or fill her head with ideas about ghosts when she lived all alone and was already starting to get old.

But a few years later, something happened that changed Dad's mind. By this time, he and Mum had got married. Robbie was a toddler and I was a baby. Granny had a problem with her house. There was water running into the sitting room, through the back wall. The house is on a slight slope, and it seemed that some old spring had opened up in the hillside, and water was coming into the house.

It was really upsetting for Granny. She had to fight with the insurance people. Dad says you pay insurers to do just one thing, but when it's finally time for them to do what they promised, they do everything that they can to get out of paying up.

And there were workers crawling all over the place – drainage specialists, engineers – trying to figure out where the water was coming in and how to fix it. But no one could, so Granny was very worried.

Dad left Mum at home with me and Robbie, and went to see if he could help. I mean, there was nothing he could do about the water problem, but he could at least be there to support Granny. So Dad went and stayed for the weekend, and that Saturday afternoon, Granny took a phone call.

Even though it was a Saturday, two workers were still poking around in the garden using special radar that can see into the ground, trying to find the route the water was taking into the house.

"Yes," Granny said into the phone, with Dad watching. "Yes, if you can. Mrs Bromley told me about you. Yes. Today? Yes, if you can. Oh, thank you."

She hung up and turned to Dad, smiling.

"Well, I know you'll say it's silly, dear," Granny said, "but I heard about this lady from Jean Bromley. She's a water diviner. A dowser.

She can find water, where it's hiding ... She's going to come over."

At three o'clock, the woman arrived. Dad said he didn't know what he'd been expecting really – maybe some old lady with a red handkerchief wrapped around her head and too much silver jewellery. But the woman was very ordinary looking. Dad said she was dressed as if she was an estate agent or something.

Anyway, the lady walked around the garden for five minutes, smiling at the workers. Then she came back over and said to Granny, "They're looking in the wrong place – there's a stream underground that runs along the side of the garden, and then, under the terrace, there's a small reservoir. It's blocked, and the stream is backing up and is coming through your sitting-room wall instead."

The lady walked over to the terrace and stamped with her foot where she said the hidden reservoir was. The workers came over with their radar, shaking their heads and smirking until they got their equipment running. Then they stopped smirking because everything the water diviner had said turned out to be true. She had solved in a moment the problem a dozen experts had not been able to solve in months.

Granny smiled. "Oh, thank you so much," she said in that simple way of hers. 'I'm so relieved. Now, you've come a long way, would you like a cup of tea?"

So they went inside and sat in the old, low-beamed dining room, chatting about this and that. Then the woman looked first at Dad and then at Granny and said, "Now, I don't want to alarm you, but tell me, who is the old man in a black suit sitting by the fireplace?"

Dad just stared. He said he went cold all over and just stared.

Granny got all excited at the idea she had a ghost living with her and wasn't scared one bit. She said the cottage was very old and she didn't really know who had lived in it before her. It certainly wasn't Dad's dad, her husband, because he had never worn a suit in his life.

Dad just stared at the fireplace, and when he got home, he told Mum what had happened and how the water diviner had seen exactly the same person Mum had, five years earlier. Dad said he was sorry, and then he went quiet, because he was remembering all the "other things" Mum had said she'd seen, things he hadn't believed. This included things Dad didn't want to believe, things they still have never told me. Mum and Dad say that Robbie and I are too young to hear certain stories.

So Dad changed his mind about Mum being able to see ghosts – or rather, he had his mind changed for him. He says, in his defence, he had never had any experience with ghosts, so it wasn't his fault he didn't believe in them. But Mum says it just shows you should never think you know everything and that other people might know things you don't.

But Dad's still not happy about Mum seeing ghosts. I think it's cool, and Robbie doesn't seem to care either way, but Dad ... there's something about it that bothers him. It bothers him a lot. I don't think it's that he's scared – it's something else.

I think Dad should be pleased. He should celebrate Mum's gift. I mean, it's largely what her books were about – what she wrote about, I mean. Mum used to write novels, but she was not doing so great as a writer until she started weaving in bits of stories about ghosts – things she had seen and felt for herself. Then her books really took off.

The publishers said that it was down to the publicity – people loved that these were "real" ghost stories, even if Mum created them as novels, changing things to make the story better and so on. So really, Dad should thank Mum, and the ghosts too, because for a while, when I was young, she was earning quite a lot of money from them.

*

And now Dad has lost his job. And not just him – his company sacked eight hundred people without warning. They sacked the entire staff and are going to replace them all with agency workers. Dad says they are people who will be employed without proper contracts, employed by the hour, as and when they're needed. They're paid way less money and won't have any decent employment rights.

And not only that, but no one even showed up from the company when it happened. None of the directors came. They just had everyone join a video call at nine o'clock last Thursday morning. Then this man in a suit, who no one had even ever met before, sacked them. He told them to leave the building and go straight home. There and then. Eight hundred people, eight hundred families, just like ours, without enough money coming in, with no way of knowing how to survive.

I wonder how many of those eight hundred families are dealing with it by going on holiday and wandering over the empty Yorkshire hills, going to spread their granny's ashes on the landscape.

A landscape full of ghosts, Mum says, though she hasn't seen one.

And strangely, it turns out it's not her who sees a ghost first.

It's me.

THREE

This morning was one of those mornings. Everyone was cross with each other. Again.

"I didn't even like that damn job," Dad said. "I didn't do it because I *wanted* to do it, I did it because I *had* to."

No one answered him.

We were sitting at the breakfast table. We're staying in a pub with guest rooms, right on the River Cover. It's just where the Cover meets the River Ure. Dad chose it because there's the ruin of a watermill a short way upstream, along the Ure. It's called Danby High Mill.

Dad wanted to see the ruin because it's where his great-grandfather, Alfred, was born. We spent some of the day there earlier in the week, in the rain. And then we drove a short way and poked around another ruined place, called Coverham Mill. This one had been a water-powered sawmill. It's where Alfred's father had been born. He was called Thomas.

While we walked around, Dad talked about all these relatives – these huge families of nine, twelve, fourteen people, all living and working around the mills. Dad had a printout of his family tree with him. *Our* family tree, I suppose.

It was several sheets of A4. He started it after we came last year, but now it's grown and grown. Dad had printed it all out and stuck all the sheets of A4 together, and he was talking about great-grandmothers and great-great-aunts as if they meant something to us.

I took one look at his printout, to keep him happy, and saw that he'd continued it right up until the present day. There he was on the family tree, married to Mum, and he'd marked in Robbie being born. But as usual Dad hadn't got as far as including me.

I wasn't surprised. It's the same with baby photos. There are thousands of Robbie and hardly any of me. When Robbie was born, Dad bought a digital camera and got into photography, but by the time I came along, he was bored of that. The only baby photos of me were on a phone that Mum had, but she dropped it in the river when I fell in last time we were here. She hadn't backed her phone up, so that was that.

I saw I was missing from the family tree, and I just shrugged and walked off to poke around the mill, the one where Alfred had been born. He was my great-great-grandfather, but that meant nothing to me. I mean, it's so long ago. Dad had said Alfred was born in 1859, I think. But it was strange, standing there in the ruins of the mill, thinking about it.

I looked around. The mill barely looked like a building any longer. Just a pile of stones, really, some of the walls still half-standing, the roof long gone. There were trees growing up from the rubble inside the building, and they were large trees – that must mean the roof fell in decades ago.

I tried to imagine that it had once had a roof and that it wasn't all falling down, covered in ivy and hidden in the wild undergrowth. That it had been a real place with real people living there. Working there. It was a corn mill, Dad had told us. They milled grain using a waterwheel that was powered by the river water. It was hard to imagine. Then I tried to imagine that I was related to these people, that they were my family, but that ... that was impossible.

*

Then things got worse. At breakfast this morning, I mean. We had nearly finished and were about to get ready to go out for the day. But the TV was on in the pub dining room, and it was the morning news. The story about Dad's company was on. The owner of the company was explaining why they'd sacked everyone. He was dressed in a very smart suit, and his hair was brushed very carefully to one side. As he talked, he smiled a smile that hovered around his lips and had nothing to do with his eyes.

"In the modern, competitive business world, we sometimes have to make tough decisions," the owner said. "The company has acted responsibly by releasing the workforce. With this act, the future of the company is assured, and these workers are now free to pursue whatever employment opportunities they wish."

Dad stared open-mouthed at the TV.

"Can you believe this guy?" he said, red in the face. "'Assured the company's future?' What he means is he's assured *his* future. Assured his chance to own a yacht in the Mediterranean and buy his kids quad bikes for Christmas!"

Mum put her hand on Dad's.

"Shush, love," she said. "Don't upset yourself."

"But ..." Dad spluttered, waving a hand at the TV set. "Did you hear what he said? I'm 'free to pursue other employment opportunities'. What a load of—"

"I know," said Mum. "But it's done now. There's no point holding on to the past."

"It's easy for him to say that," said Dad. "Look at him! Probably went to some fancy private school, then Oxford ... All nice and easy with his daddy's money. Someone like that ... he's probably never had to worry about paying a bill in his entire life!"

"Yeah," said Robbie, "but you know, it's not his fault he's a—"

Robbie said the rudest word then, and Mum got cross for a second. She tried to be angry, but then she just started crying, because she hates it when Robbie swears. And that's something he's doing more and more.

The other thing that Robbie is doing more and more is not talking to me.

I don't know why. He just goes quiet at me for no reason. One day I overheard Mum telling Dad that it's because of Robbie's age – that it's normal to get moody, to want to be by himself, that kind of stuff. But I don't know, it seems like there's more to it than that. Now Robbie will only talk to me if Mum insists, and then Dad gets angry at Mum for making Robbie do something he doesn't want to.

He's been doing it again all morning. Robbie hasn't said a word to me, even though we're sharing a room in the pub, just down the corridor from Mum and Dad's. He didn't even say anything when we sat in the back seat of the car together as we travelled to Crackpot Hall again.

As we pulled up in the car park, a little thing happened – an old lady fell over. Mum rushed to help her and picked her up, got her sitting. Dad came over and asked if she'd like us to call an ambulance, but she said she was fine. Just shaken up.

I think she was embarrassed more than anything, but Mum chatted to her for a while – asked her questions about where she lived and who her family was. Before long, the lady was smiling and on her feet again, toddling away to get on with her day.

Then we started out. And like I said, I was soon left behind.

*

Dad's leading the way, Mum a little further behind him, and Robbie?

Half the time, Robbie is like a Labrador or something else that's over-excited. He goes ahead, then comes back, then slows, then runs ahead again. From time to time, Mum snaps at him as he clambers on large boulders by the side of the path, or stares down at the drop over a bridge.

"Robbie! Be careful!" Mum cries into the brisk wind, but he doesn't listen to her, just as he doesn't listen to me.

I've been walking slower and slower. By the time I reach Crackpot Hall, the other three are way up the track that leads further up the hillside.

That's when I see the ghost.

At least, I don't think it's a ghost to start with. And I don't see her. I *hear* her. I hear her laughter – the sound of a young girl laughing. It's not a mean laugh – it's a cheeky one. A laugh full of fun and mischief. As if she's spying on me and knows that I can't see her. The laugh seems to dance around me. Finally, I realise that the sound is bouncing off the various broken walls and stones of the Hall.

"Hello?" I call out.

No answer for a moment. Then more laughter.

"I know you're there," I say, which is dumb. I don't know anything. I don't know who it is, and I don't know where she is, either. Then I look for the others, but they're long out of sight. So I go into the ruins of the Hall again, just like we did a year ago.

Unlike a year ago, the place is not deserted. There is someone else there. A young girl. Maybe she's seven or eight. She's standing still, staring, as if she was just waiting for me to come and find her. She's dressed strangely, I can see that at once. Something about her already makes the hairs on the back of my neck stand up and a prickle run down my spine like someone is scraping their fingernail along it.

Her clothes are old. I mean really old. They are old like the clothes in the ancient, fuzzy black-and-white photos of people we were looking at in a visitor's centre the other day. People from the nineteenth century, when photography had only just been invented. That was when you had to stand still for thirty seconds or something to make the photograph, or it would be blurry.

As all of that is sinking in, she laughs again. There is a magical light that dances in her eyes when she smiles.

Then she speaks.

"Follow me," she says. She turns and walks right through the stone wall – there one minute and walking through solid stone the next.

I hear her voice again, "Follow me!" and the laughter.

And what do I do?

I run for dear life, run away, out of the Hall and up the path, while her laughter rings in my ears, and her voice.

"Follow me!"

FOUR

As I run, I realise I already know who the girl is.

She's one of the wild children.

Dad told us about them. A couple of days ago, he was reading aloud from an old book he'd bought in a second-hand bookshop. The book was written so long ago, but it had a description of all the walks you could do in the area. There was a short passage in it about Crackpot Hall – and back then, people still lived there, although the roof of the house had already started to sag.

The foundations of the house had begun to slip, and the doors and windows weren't straight any longer. The book said the floors inside sloped like the deck of a ship at sea. But Dad also read out this: "The children at Crackpot Hall are untamed like their home. They are spirits of the moors, running barefoot. Wild children."

The girl I've just seen was barefoot. She was wild and untamed, just like the hills around her – a wild landscape. She must be one of the children the book was talking about, but the book is over a hundred years old.

I shiver as I run, and I keep glancing back to see if she's following me. But there's nothing there. No one.

I'm getting tired, and I still haven't caught up with the others, so I slow to a walk and plod along the path. I'm wondering how they can have got so far ahead of me again, wondering why they don't wait for me. Ever.

I think it's because Mum and Dad are both only children. They say it makes you more grown up, being an only child. I don't know if that's true, but Mum and Dad both think so. I think it means they don't really understand what it's like to be the younger brother, never quite able to keep up with Robbie, or with anyone.

Finally, I come down a little track that crosses a stream that runs along the bottom of a gulley. Above, on the far side, I see the three of them, standing, looking at another building.

This one is large but even more of a ruin than Crackpot Hall.

I'm about to start running again, to run up and tell them I saw a ghost, but then I stop myself.

I'm not sure why.

I come closer, watching the three of them. They haven't seen me, and I'm close enough now to see that they're reading a plaque that's been fixed to the side of the ruined building. The three of them have their backs to me, and as I come up, Robbie runs off.

Mum and Dad still haven't seen me. They wander away from the sign, and as they do, they start talking about Robbie.

I stop, not knowing whether to say hello or listen.

"You have to stop going on at Robbie, making him talk to James," says Dad. "It won't help anything."

"But he can't just forget about his brother!" says Mum.

"Look," says Dad, "who decides what Robbie should do? He's a teenage boy, with teenage-boy problems. He can't cope with James on top of everything else."

Suddenly I feel bad. I shouldn't let Mum and Dad talk without knowing I can hear. But they're talking about *me*. I hesitate for a moment, wondering if I should go over and demand to know what they're saying about me. I don't. Instead, I back away and go and read the sign that they were looking at:

Abandoned Lead Mine

This is all that is left of a local industry – lead mining.

Look around you. The landscape may seem natural, but it is not. Lead ore was once mined in the hills of Swaledale. Do you see the long grooves running down the hillside behind you? These are not natural features.

The miners had different ways of taking out the lead ore. One way was to dam a stream or spring on the hilltop and make

*an artificial lake. Then the dam would be
breached, and the flood of water would
rush down the hillside. It made these
vast grooves in the ground and revealed
the lead ore in the process.*

I do what the sign says and turn around,
and, yes, there are these huge gashes in the
hillside. It's like a gigantic animal has scraped
the earth away with its claws. Now that I see
them, I realise that they are dotted all over this
landscape. Dozens of them. It's amazing. The
place is so empty, so desolate, but the size and
number of these grooves show that once it was
very, very busy. Once upon a time the place
must have been crawling with people. It's hard
to imagine. I can only sort of feel it.

The sign isn't finished yet:

*This was hard work, but it was preferable
to the other way that lead was taken – by
digging mineshafts into the hillsides, far
underground.*

*Working these mines was dangerous. As
well as the long-term health issues of*

*working with lead, which is poisonous,
the mine shafts sometimes collapsed, and
deaths from such events were common.*

*The men who mined the seams of lead
ore were called "orewinners". Those
who dragged the useless rock away were
called "deadmen".*

*The average life expectancy for a mine
worker was just forty-five. Boys as young
as ten or eleven were sent into the mines
to drag carts of lead ore back out to the
open air.*

*Once, this landscape was a hive of human
activity, with lead mines found all across
the area. From here, lead was shipped
across the country and across the world.*

I turn away from the sign again and try to
picture what it was like for boys of about my age
to work in a tiny tunnel far, far underground,
with the orewinners and the deadmen. But
again, I can't imagine it. I can't see it. I can't
picture it. There's just a feeling that scrapes up
the back of my head.

I wander back over to Mum. Dad has disappeared, and Mum just stares at the ground, not looking at me as she talks.

"James, love ... Jamie," she says. "I'm sorry if you heard any of that. We all ... love you, OK?"

I don't say anything.

"It's just all really hard at the moment," Mum goes on. "With, you know ... everything. And Dad's job."

"It's OK, Mum," I say. "I under—"

"And I still don't know why I can't write," she says, interrupting me. "But I can't. It just went."

I don't say anything, because I have no idea how to help Mum with her not writing any more. But it seems like she doesn't need me to say anything – she just wants someone to listen to her, and right now, that someone is me. That feels like something good at least. Something I can do. So I sit down and listen.

"For years, I didn't even have to think about it. There were so many stories to tell, so many ideas, and it was easy. I just did it. And then it stopped. People always talk about writing like a well emptying or a spring drying up. One minute there's water flowing, without any effort. And the next minute it's just gone. The well is dry. I suppose I just never thought it would happen to me. And I have no idea why."

Then Mum starts to cry, very softly, and I feel awful.

I reach out to her, but then I hesitate. I don't know whether to hug her or not. I wonder if I could cheer her up by telling her about the ghost, but still something stops me.

And then Dad and Robbie are coming back.

Dad knows what to do. He wraps his big arms around Mum and just holds her for a long while.

Robbie stands looking at them sadly.

Then Dad pulls away.

"Come on," he says, "let's get this walk done. Spread these ashes. Then get off this hillside before the rain comes."

I look out across the hills. It's still sunny, but I see Dad's right to move us on. There are tall white clouds on the horizon, swelling and lifting up high into the atmosphere. The clouds are white, but their centres are darkening, grey. They have rain in them – even I can see that.

Dad's still talking as we go.

"You know what? When we've done this, we should go and have fish and chips or something? Right? We *are* on holiday, after all."

So we walk on, but I just stay silent.

I don't tell them about the wild girl ghost. It feels like something just for me, for now at least. I feel guilty because Mum wants to see ghosts, but I can't help myself. This ghost is mine – this one is just for me. But as we walk on, a surprising thought pops into my head.

I wish I'd gone with her. When the ghost said, "Follow me," I shouldn't have been afraid. I should have gone. I promise myself that if I ever see her again, I'll follow.

FIVE

I'm trying to keep up with Mum and Dad and Robbie when I suddenly realise I have seen her before. The ghost girl. I have seen her in a dream.

Last night, I had this strange dream, although it took me a while to realise I was dreaming.

There was just blackness, and I didn't know where I was. I opened my eyes, and I couldn't see anything – I mean literally nothing, not even a faint glimmer of light. And that was odd, because in the room Robbie and I are sharing, I've always seen the glow of the streetlight that stands at one end of the bridge where the road crosses the River Cover.

But last night there was nothing, and then I realised that I was not in the bedroom with Robbie, above the pub. Not only was there no light, but the sound was wrong too. It wasn't the close, soft space of a bedroom that I was in. Instead, I could sense a cold, hard and very large space around me. The world was gone. Time stopped. There was only me. Me and the blackness.

It was weird, because it was then that I realised I was dreaming, but still I didn't wake up. I just watched the dream unfold like it was a film that I was watching. A film that I was in.

I was in a cave. I could hear running water, but not close. And it wasn't a trickle of water – it was a roaring torrent, but far, far away. The sound was like a distant rush of white noise, angry and fierce, just a long way in the distance.

I felt cold, and I sensed the mass of rock all around me, above and below me. I knew somehow that I was far underground. I was sure of it. I didn't need to be told, or to be shown it. I just knew it, in the way that you often do just know things in dreams that you wouldn't really be able to know.

Suddenly, a girl was there, in front of me.

The wild child.

I didn't realise it when I saw her back at Crackpot Hall, but now, as I try to catch up to Mum, Dad and Robbie, it comes to me. She is the girl from my dream, and in my dream, she was a little way away, maybe twenty or thirty metres or something. The wild child was the only thing I could see. It wasn't like she was glowing, or that there was a light shining on her from somewhere like a spotlight. I could just see her. Her and nothing else.

She wasn't facing me. She had her back to me, and she started to move. I knew I was supposed to follow her, and I did. Because I knew it was a dream, I knew I didn't need to be scared. Nothing can harm you in a dream, right? It's like taking part in a film – it's not real, it can't hurt me, nothing can hurt me. I knew all that, so I followed the girl, and she didn't walk but somehow she moved, and I was moving too, also without walking.

I got closer. I caught her up and was beside her. We were moving forward together, side by side, in the darkness. She was a young girl, and she was shorter than me, but I somehow knew she was way more powerful than I was.

Without looking at me, she spoke.

41

"Do you know who you are?" she asked.

That's all she said, and yet there was something about the way she said it that terrified me, and I woke up screaming.

At least I thought I did. I sat bolt upright in bed and I was convinced I was screaming, but I wasn't. I must have just dreamed that I was, because Robbie was lying there, asleep, undisturbed, his shape under the duvet just visible in the orange glow from the streetlight.

My heart pounded, as hard as if I had really just been screaming. I thought about waking Robbie up, but I stopped myself. Because ... what was I going to say to him? He was just going to be grumpy I'd woken him, so I lay back down and stared at the ceiling. Before I forgot, I repeated what the ghost girl, the wild child, had asked me.

Have you ever noticed that when you dream something, no matter how strong it feels at the time, you think you're going to remember it? But the moment you go back to sleep, or wake up the next day, it's gone. And I knew this was important, so as I went back to sleep, I repeated to myself, over and over and over: "Do you know who you are, do you know who you are?"

SIX

As we walk on, I realise I am trailing further and further behind the others again.

I know we have to hurry, and I know we must scatter Granny's ashes today. Tomorrow, we'll get back in the car and drive home, to who knows what? To Dad looking for work and Mum worrying about how we will make ends meet. Mum said she can try to ask for more hours at the arts centre, but she's not hopeful. So we have to do as Granny wished, and we have to get that done before the rain comes in. Even as I trudge onwards, I see that the clouds are thicker than before, clustering on the horizon, filling the sky.

I should tell Mum that I saw a ghost.

It seems to be all that she thinks about now. I am guessing Mum thinks that if she sees a ghost, it might start her writing again. She thinks she has a need to see something other

43

than the boring ordinary world around her – that she is tired of it, that she wants there to be, well … *more*.

More to all of this, this life we fall into and fall out of without any control over those two things. Mum wants to believe the world means something, she wants to feel the urge to write again, because that is what makes her feel that *she* means something. I could really help her by telling her about the wild child.

"Mum," I'll say. "I saw a ghost."

And she'll say, "Where? When?" When I tell her it was back at Crackpot Hall, she'll ask me why I didn't tell her at the time. Robbie will laugh at me and tell me I'm making it up, and Dad … I know how Dad will react. I think that's why I don't want to say it. Dad can hardly stand it that Mum sees things – ghosts, I mean. And if I start saying I'm seeing them too …

He gets this look in his eyes, does Dad. A sort of sad, sort of disappointed look, and I don't want to see it. *That's* why I haven't said anything.

I want to please Mum, but I don't want to upset Dad. And then there's Robbie. I hate it when he makes fun of me. But right now, I just wish he would talk to me at all.

Yesterday, with the bad weather stopping us from going on walks, or doing anything much outside, we visited a stately home. On the way there, it was the same thing with Robbie – I tried talking to him a couple of times, but he didn't even reply. I didn't bother moaning to Mum or Dad to get him to answer. I knew it wouldn't work, and it was the same as we trailed around the stately home.

A funny thing happened there. Strange, I mean.

The place was called Danewick Manor. This is the real deal, unlike Crackpot Hall, which is just some old farm up on the dale. It's a huge place, very grand. I zoned out when Mum was talking about when it was built. I hate places like that. Or rather, it's not that I hate them, it's that I hate trailing around them. It's boring, for one thing, and for another, I think they're depressing, though I can't figure out why.

We were walking down a wide and endless corridor. Mum and Dad were up ahead, stopping at this painting, or that sculpture, reading the little plaques that explain what everything is and who's in the paintings, and so on.

Robbie was on his phone, and despite the fact there was barely any signal, he kept checking it as if it was suddenly going to start working properly again. I guessed he was messaging some mates from school.

"This place must cost a fortune to run," said Mum, looking around her.

"My heart bleeds for them," said Dad, and he gave a short, harsh laugh. "There's a nice council flat for sale down the road from us. Maybe they could move there instead."

"Don't be like that," Mum said.

"Like what?" said Dad. "This place is still in private hands, isn't it? They can't be that hard up."

"They've had to open it up to the public, for paying visitors."

"Like I said," Dad muttered. "My heart just bleeds. Having to let scum like us in here."

I pulled away. They moved on, but I stopped and stared out of a window.

It was one of those old latticed windows, made up of lots of little diamond shapes. I stared through just one of these little diamonds, down across the parkland of the manor.

Something grabbed my attention. Beyond the formal gardens of the manor, beyond the parkland, I could just make out the ruin of something in the trees. Then I realised, we'd been there already – it was the ruined watermill, the one on the Ure. The one where Alfred, Dad's great-grandfather, had been born, where he lived, where he worked. His family must have worked the mill that supplied this manor – maybe they even worked for them. I don't know.

I was suddenly struck by a funny thought – that the place my family used to call home is a ruin covered in ivy, while this place is still standing in all its grandeur. Even if they do have to let the paying public in to see it.

I turned to Mum and Dad and was going to tell them – I didn't know if they knew our ruined watermill was just down there. But as I opened my mouth, Dad spoke.

To be accurate, he swore.

He was bending over, reading the little plaque underneath a painting.

"Ha. So that's him," he said quietly. "The bastard."

"William," said Mum. "Don't swear, for God's sake."

Dad just stared at her. Things are happening inside Dad that I do not understand. And I am not sure he understands them either.

I started to go up to him, to make sure everything was OK between him and Mum. But as I approached, he flicked a finger in the face of the man in the painting. He didn't hit it hard, but just Dad's luck, as he did it, one of the guides in the manor came around the corner at the far end of the hall. She saw him do it.

"Sir?" said the woman, who started bustling down the corridor towards him like a grumpy steam train.

Dad rolled his eyes.

"Sir!" said the guide again, more forcefully this time.

Dad looked at her for a moment as she arrived, grumpily.

"Sir, did I see you strike that portrait?"

I could see Dad was working out which way to go with his reply.

"Strike?" he asked.

"You attacked the portrait, sir," said the woman, her mouth a thin line.

"*Attacked* it? I brushed it with my finger. There was some dust on it. You should do a better job of cleaning these old *relics*."

Dad emphasised that last word, and with that he jabbed a thumb at the man in the painting.

"Sir, I clearly saw you attempting to damage this portrait, and I will have to ask you to leave the premises."

"Gladly," said Dad, with a forced smile. He turned and marched down the hallway. As he went, he shouted, "I've had enough of this. I'm waiting in the car."

I stared at Dad's back.

Then I looked at the painting, wondering what had upset Dad so much.

It was a painting of a soldier. Not just any soldier, an officer of some kind. It was a formal painting, one of those weird things where he's in uniform but standing in some strange imaginary landscape of mountains, by a chair with rugs on it. There were two hunting dogs at the soldier's feet.

It was certainly ridiculous, but I didn't see why it made Dad so furious.

Mum had wandered off, embarrassed. Robbie was staring out of the window. The guide stared at them both, still angry, but there was nothing she could really do about them. She wasn't taking any notice of me at all, so I read the plaque:

Major General Sir Clive Seacope

It affected Dad so much that he didn't talk again for the rest of the day, but it meant nothing to me. Nothing at all. It was only later, at tea-time, that I found out what had bothered him so much.

SEVEN

Yesterday evening, things still weren't good. Not even OK.

After tea in the pub, Mum announced that she wanted to go for a walk. I didn't want her to go off alone, but no one else tried to stop her. So I tried to start a conversation. There was a poster for a band on the noticeboard of the pub. It said they were called Steel and Wool and that they were playing here the next night – tonight, our last night. They looked like a folk band. I don't even like folk music, but I figured it was something we could do together, all of us, something easy.

"That might be fun," I said, trying to get Mum to talk about it so she would stay with me.

She didn't. She simply got up, and Dad just watched as she left.

Robbie sighed and said he was going to our room to play on his console, and I stayed sitting, while Dad stared into space.

I didn't know what to say. I stared at the poster a bit more.

Dad sighed and reached down into his shoulder bag on the floor. He pulled out more of his large sheets of paper, pushing our empty plates to one side, and unfolded the family tree he's been making.

"Help me, Jamie," he said very quietly, staring at his sheets of paper. So I went and slid onto the bench next to him.

"Such big families in our history," Dad said, and he ran his finger down the branches of the tree. "Such huge families. Fifteen of them here at Coverham Sawmill. Eighteen of them at Danby. And it's the same in other branches of the family too. This lot here – the Raws. That's a funny name, isn't it? I'm sure I've seen it somewhere before ..."

He stopped speaking and pulled out his laptop, connecting it to the pub Wi-Fi.

Dad pulled up the ancestry site he's been using and started searching again. Then he opened a spreadsheet he's made, where he's listing all our relatives.

I was watching him, but I didn't know how to help, so I just sat close to him and listened.

"That name ..." Dad started to say.

He tapped something into the website, and then stared at his spreadsheet again, and finally at his sheets of paper stuck together – the family tree.

"Well, I'll be ..." Dad said, his voice trailing off for a moment. He ran his hand through his hair and then he went on. "Rachel Raw. Rachel. She's my – let me think – my great-great-grandmother. Bloody hell, according to this, she lived at Crackpot Hall! Ha ha! That's fantastic. Now I know why it feels like it means something to me. It must be in my blood!"

Dad was suddenly so excited.

"Can you believe that? I'm related to someone from Crackpot!"

I stared at Dad's map, his tree of family names, and I read. All these Sarahs and Josephs.

Roberts and Williams. Alices and Elizabeths, Eleanors and Rachels ... *Who are they? I wondered. Why does any of this matter? They're all long gone, and all I care about is my family, here and now, and that no one in it can seem to speak to each other any more. Isn't that what matters?*

Dad traced his finger across the tree.

"And then Rachel moves to Coverham Sawmill. I guess she fell in love with Thomas, my great-great-grandfather. And then we get to Alfred at Danby High Mill, and then ..."

Dad sat back with a sigh.

"Then they're all gone," he said quietly. He wasn't really speaking to me; he was just thinking out loud. "No more large families. After that they live in ones and twos, and they're not in the countryside any more – they're in Liverpool, Leeds. Manchester, Preston. Anywhere that will have them ..."

He rubbed his eyes with his thumb and forefinger. Pulling his glass towards him, Dad downed the end of the beer he'd been nursing since dinner.

I was about to speak. I wanted to say something, but I just felt so lost, so useless, so clumsy. That's the way I feel almost all the time these days, it seems.

Dad stared at the ceiling.

"James," he said, "Jamie. I can't believe I'm saying this, but help your mother, won't you?"

I didn't know what he meant. *That's so unfair*, I thought. *I always help – always, without them even asking. It's Robbie they have to keep nagging, to get him to clear the table, or tidy his room, or whatever. They nag him, and he doesn't do it, and yet he's still the golden boy. And I do everything I can, without even being asked, and now Dad's telling me to help?*

I was really feeling mad, but before I could say anything, the door to the pub opened and Mum came back in.

She wandered over to the table.

"Sorry, love," she said to Dad. "Just needed some air ... you know."

Dad held her hand and smiled a weak smile. "I know. I know."

"It's nice by the bridge – it's a warm evening. Come and sit for a bit before bed."

They got up and went out, but I hesitated a moment before following. Dad had packed his stuff up and taken it with him, but it was as if I could still see it spread out on the table before me. I wondered why it was that with all these names, all this history, I didn't feel like I belonged to any of it.

After a while, I wandered outside and found Mum and Dad sitting on the low wall of the stone bridge that arches over the river. The sun was just setting behind the trees. I was still feeling upset about Dad telling me to help Mum when I was always trying to help them both. But I let it go because Dad was explaining to Mum why he got angry at the manor house we visited.

It turned out that Dad had discovered that the man in the painting was the one responsible for closing the mill his family worked in.

"Nothing so strange in that," he said. "It happened to lots of families. As soon as there's a cheaper way to do something, that's what people do. They do it the new way, the cheaper way, so they can make more money. They don't care how many people lose their jobs or their homes as a result."

I was about to say something when Dad said it for me.

"You know what happened to me last week? My job?" he sighed. "It's exactly the same story, just a hundred and fifty years later …"

They sat in silence for a moment, and I was pleased to see Mum reach out and hold Dad's hand.

"The weather's better this evening," she said.

Dad looked up at the sky.

"Yes, well," he said. "It has to stay that way. We only have tomorrow to scatter the ashes."

"I know, love," said Mum.

"Are you sure you want to come?" asked Dad. "I mean, I know it's—"

"No," said Mum, interrupting. "It's fine. I want to go up there too."

*

So that's where we still are, spread out like four lonely ants, on this vast hillside, chasing ghosts. And the rain is coming in.

EIGHT

Finally, I catch up with Mum, Dad and Robbie again.

I can't work it out.

Mum and Dad seem to be fighting. At least, not fighting, but they're not speaking. I can't work out why one minute they're fine and the next there's this awful tension between them.

One thing is the same: Robbie is in a foul mood. I know he doesn't want to be here, but I don't know what he'd rather do. It seems like nothing makes him happy any more. Not like he used to be. Not like we used to be.

Robbie and I used to have such a laugh, always messing around, making silly jokes, acting crazy, just giggling at anything and everything. That's all gone now. I can't stand it.

The three of them are standing on a bend as I reach them. I catch the end of what Dad's saying, even if he's only saying it to himself.

"I still can't work it out," says Dad, staring at his map. "Crackpot Hall is back down here, but the village of Crackpot is over six miles away. Over there …"

He points and then adds, "It doesn't make sense."

Robbie doesn't reply and neither does Mum.

I look at them both and go and stand next to Dad. I don't know what to say, but at least doing that might make him feel like someone is interested in him, in what he has to say.

Dad shrugs and we walk on. As we do, I think about Crackpot Hall again, getting further away with every step. I think about the wild child, my ghost. And as I think about her, I suddenly realise that she could be a relative of mine. One of Dad's ancestors, who lived at Crackpot.

I regret not following her when she appeared before. Maybe that was my one chance. More than ever, I decide to keep this as my secret. It's something for me, and I *need* something. I can't really explain it, I just feel as if I am floating further and further away from my family.

Then things get worse because it starts raining.

When it comes, it comes fast. It was a bright morning when we set out, but as predicted, the clouds have rolled over the whole sky now, and the light has changed. A gentle drizzle starts, and Mum and Dad start bickering again about why we left late this morning.

"Can't we just go home?" says Robbie, moaning. "I just want to go home!"

They ignore him. They keep walking, and Robbie drags further behind with each step.

And then, for the first time in ages, he talks to me. No, he doesn't talk – he shouts.

"Jamie, this is all your fault!" Robbie yells angrily. He spits the words back at me without even looking, but I can see his face in my mind, all chewed up.

"Why is it my fault?" I say. "You're the one in a mood all the time!"

Robbie doesn't answer.

He just puts his head down, pulls his anorak up and marches along after Mum and Dad.

"I hate you!" Robbie shouts. "I hate you so much!"

I watch him go.

The rain falls on me. It falls on Robbie, and somewhere ahead it falls on Mum and Dad. It falls on Crackpot Hall. It falls on Swaledale. It falls on Yorkshire. Nothing escapes.

I stare at Robbie's back, and suddenly I break.

I have had enough.

I will show them – I have no idea what, but I will. I turn off the main path and start to jog down a tiny, snaking little track, barely wide enough to put one foot beside the other. Then I start to run, stumbling as I go.

I run, blindly, into the rain, down into the valley, taking turns without thinking. I'm heading nowhere, with nothing in my head but the pain. The pain of rejection.

The rain gets harder, and I start to feel cold, but I keep running. Ahead I see a stream that cuts down a gulley. I head towards it and then, as I move to jump the stream, my foot slips on the wet rock. I half-fall, half-slide into the stream, into a pool. The shock of the cold water hits me a moment after I enter the water, and I feel pain. Pain from my knee and from my head. I have hit them both.

I try to clamber out of the pool I've fallen in and make a mess of it. But then I succeed, and I stagger up and out of the water, bending over, sobbing, shivering.

Then I stop.

I stop because I am aware that someone is standing in front of me, someone who has appeared from nowhere.

I lift my head, and it is the wild child.

"I need your help," she says.

I just stare at her. I know she is a ghost, but she looks so real, so very real.

"I need your help," she says again.

Her clothes are as before: old, strange. Her hair is short.

"There's a boy," she says. "He's trapped. You have to help. Follow me."

And this time, I do.

NINE

The girl hurries ahead of me. As we go, I call out questions.

"Where are we going?"

"What's your name?"

"Who is this boy? Where is he? Is he hurt?"

She doesn't answer. Either she can't hear me, or she chooses to ignore me. She's half-running, half-scurrying, hopping over the larger stones that sometimes block the path, heading upwards again now.

The rain is getting harder and harder, and I feel as if I am soaked to the skin. But I have stopped shivering – the run has warmed me up, and my anger with my family is driving me on. This rage has suddenly burst out of nowhere, and its arrival has taken me by surprise.

I am shocked. I do not understand myself, or who I am, any longer. I don't feel much apart from this anger, but nevertheless I am curious to see where the wild child is heading.

There's a tunnel in the hillside – a tunnel so small and low that it seems hardly bigger than a rabbit warren heading into the ground. But as we get closer, I see that we can just about squeeze inside, pushing under a hanging curtain of moss and grasses and heather that almost hides the entrance.

Once we're inside, it's bigger – the ghost girl can stand upright and turn and look at me. I'm hunched over, but it's good to be out of the rain.

"Where are we?" I ask.

"Entrance to the lead mines," she says.

"It's not blocked off?" I ask, looking into the darkness ahead of me.

So these are the tunnels the miners made to get to the lead ore. Once upon a time orewinners worked at the face, extracting the precious metal, while deadmen carted the useless rock away. Now there is nothing.

"That depends," the girl says in answer to my question, and laughs.

I don't know what she means.

"And this boy is down there?" I ask.

"Aye," she says. "He is."

"How will we see in the dark? Maybe we should go back? If he's hurt, we should go and get help. My mum and dad are somewhere nearby, I think."

The girl looks at me.

Then she turns and heads down the tunnel.

"Wait!" I cry. "Stop!"

She doesn't.

I pull my mobile from my pocket. I'm not going to call anyone – I know there's no reception up here – but I type a text to Dad and send it. Or I try to anyway, just in case it gets through somehow. I tell Dad where I am, where I *think* I am. And what I'm doing. But that makes me realise I have no idea what I'm doing.

I'm going underground, I type. *Somewhere in the valley. I'm going to rescue someone.*

Then I turn on the torch – the real reason I took my phone out. I head after her, hoping I charged the battery overnight. I can't remember.

She hasn't got far. She's at a gate set into the rock.

It's made of wood and is heavy, but I can see it's rotting in places. Without waiting for me, the girl drifts through a narrow crack between two slats of the gate which have rotted at the ends, freeing them so they swing slightly wider than the others.

She turns and looks at me.

"Hurry!" she says, but I don't see how I will get through. She reads my face and waves a hand at the old rotting gate.

"Try!" she says.

"Wait," I say. "Please just tell me one thing."

It's only now popped into my head. I don't know how I am so sure, but I feel certain I know who this is, this wild child. This ghost girl who might be a relative of Dad's. Might be? I know she is – somehow, I simply know, and I think I know exactly who, too. I'm thinking about the family tree Dad has been sketching out, bit by bit, over the months.

"Are you Rachel?" I ask. "Rachel Raw?"

Finally, she answers one of my questions.

"Aye, I'm Rachel."

"Then we're related," I say. "Somehow."

"I know that," she says, as if I'm slow. "I'm your great-great-great grandmother."

I stare at her, and for the first time since I've seen this wild child ghost girl I grow afraid. It's not possible that my great-great-great grandmother is standing here as an eight year old, talking to me in a hole in the ground in the Yorkshire landscape. But she is, and I have no time to question it further.

"There's a boy trapped," she says. "Do you understand? We have to help him. And I can't do it. I can only show you the way."

"Why can't you help him?" I ask.

"Why do you think?" she asks.

"Because ... you're a ..."

I can't say the word. The word *ghost*.

Rachel stares at me some more.

"Only you can do it," she says. She turns, and in a moment she disappears into the darkness.

TEN

We are deep underground now, a long way into the hillside, following this old mine. I wonder if it is safe, I wonder when anyone else last passed this way, but I suppose the trapped boy must have come down here.

I wonder how long he has been stuck for. If there is water he could survive some time without food, but what if he's hurt? How will I get him out? Not for the first time, I ignore the voice in my head telling me that what I am doing is foolish.

Rachel is ahead of me, almost running.

It's easy for her – she is short enough that the low ceiling of the tunnel is above her head, and anyway, I've already seen her walk through a solid stone wall. But I have to stagger, crouched over, so I don't hit my head. The miners didn't bother making the tunnel any higher than it needed to be.

I think about the boys, young boys, who hauled the lead ore out in carts and wagons from the mine face to the surface. Boys younger than me. I am suddenly struck by déjà vu – the sense that you have already seen this moment, that you have already lived it. Maybe it's because I was thinking about them, or maybe it's because of the dream I had where Rachel and I were walking underground.

It only lasts a fraction of a second, and I shake my head and press on. Rachel is moving so very fast now, and I can barely keep up. It's clear that ghosts can see in the dark, but I know I need my phone torch. I keep checking the battery indicator nervously, hoping it will last as long as … well, as long as it needs to.

At first, I don't realise that the roof of the tunnel has got higher, but then I notice I am not ducking as I was before. The ceiling has lifted, and the tunnel is wider, and then I hear a sound.

It's hard to make it out to start with, but as we head onwards, I hear this rushing noise. It is threatening and wild, and it's growing in volume all the time. Finally, I realise that it is the sound of running water – somewhere ahead in this dark space there is a violent torrent of water hurtling its way along underground passages.

Rachel stops so suddenly I almost bump into the back of her, and again I am chilled by the idea of her. Could I touch her? What would happen? Would my hand just pass right through?

The sound of the water is deafening now, and as we turn a slight corner, I see why. The space suddenly opens up into a cavern. It's huge. The miners must have accidentally hit this colossal underground space, because there is no way human hands made this cave. This is a place made by nature, or the gods.

Our little path opens up onto a ledge, and then the ground suddenly drops away down into a gulley. The roaring water comes from my left and hurtles down into this dark hole, from where the only sign it continues is the endless roar it makes, echoing back up from the depths. The outside world is long forgotten – the hills and dales of Yorkshire. Sometimes in sun, sometimes in rain. Neither ever fall in this place – this is a place outside weather, or people, or perhaps even time. It is just a total nowhere. A void.

"We have to cross," says Rachel.

I stare at her.

"Cross what?" I say, but already I see what she intends for us to do.

I shine my weak torch beam across the gulley. There are three pillars of rock that have been left behind by the carving action of the water. They stand like three stepping stones – it would be possible to use them to cross the hole. And only nature or the gods know how many millions of years it took for this to form, this terrifying space far underground. For aeons water has rushed here in total darkness, carving and smoothing the rock as it goes.

"He's across there?" I shout to Rachel, struggling to make myself heard over the sound of the tumbling water.

"We have to free him!" she cries back to me. For the first time, there's a sense of urgency about what she's saying.

I should go back, I think.

I should go back and find Mum and Dad, get them to call the emergency services. That would be the smart thing to do, but right now

I'm not feeling smart. I'm feeling like I want something for myself, something that I have done, something that makes me proud of myself. Then maybe everyone will take more notice of me, then maybe I will really become me.

So I will rescue this boy myself.

It's a foolish decision, but I don't care about being foolish right now. I just want to do something, to be something.

Rachel nods at me.

"Ready?" she shouts.

I nod.

She dances across the tops of the three pillars. That is the word for it. She just skips from the top of one pillar to the next, and there she is, on a similar ledge on the far side, turning back to wait for me. The light from my phone barely reaches her.

There is nothing for it.

I judge the distance. I am taller than Rachel, my legs longer. Where she had to skip, I can just step, from one pillar to the next, and from there to the third, which is slightly lower, I notice. I practise it in my mind. Once, twice.

"James!" Rachel cries, but the water is so loud I can barely hear her. "Come on. You can do it!"

I step. Out into the darkness. My right foot leads onto the first pillar, and I look only at where my foot is landing and not at the awful drop all around me.

I don't hesitate. *Best to do this in one motion*, I think. So I keep my momentum, and my left foot makes the second pillar top without difficulty.

One more step and I will be on the third, and I keep the flow going and reach out with my right foot. I'm going to make it, and I see Rachel waiting for me in the dark, and I know I am going to make it. But I'm wrong.

As I push off for the final time, my foot slips.

My arms swing wildly, and I cry out.

Rachel stares at me.

"James!" she cries. I see her face form a look of total horror.

Time slows to a crawl. It almost stops. I have the weird sense that I am watching myself as I fall.

My foot goes backwards on the wet pillar top. That third pillar, slightly lower than the others, is covered in spray from this underground waterfall. It's wet. I see that in the light from my mobile phone. It flies out of my hand, the light making a strange curving arc in the darkness. I have let the phone go as my arms flail wildly to get my balance, but there is no chance of steadying myself.

I watch in slow motion as I hit the pillar top on my left hip and try to grab at something, at anything, in the darkness. I cannot find anything, and my nails just scrape across cold wet rock as I fall into the terrible drop below me.

There is a sudden but dull clunk as my head hits a rock, somewhere, and then I am dropping. My phone's light has been swallowed up by the water, which I hit a moment later, and then I am gone.

I am underwater, in a waterfall dropping into the bowels of the earth. I cannot see or hear, I cannot breathe, and I am swept away.

ELEVEN

For the first thousand years, I just scream – a silent underwater scream.

For the second thousand years, I cry, and my tears are washed from my eyes by the cold, black water.

For the third thousand years, I tumble like a fragment of a leaf, down along channels and chasms, gullies and abysses. The water pulls me further and further away from everything. I am pulled by forces greater than me – I am powerless. All I can do is allow myself to be taken by these powerful forces, or I can choose to fight them, but I gave up trying to struggle long ago. I no longer even try to right myself or grasp at the rocks that I pass at speed. I am not even a leaf, but a bubble of air, no more than that. I am almost nothing.

It seems I will be dragged along by the water for ever. It feels as if those three thousand years have passed, and then another three, and yet another as I descend the hidden passages of this underground river. On and on I go, tumbling, falling, floating.

And then, with a release that is surprisingly gentle, I am washed up on a shore, the shore of a small underground pool. The water moves in this space more calmly than before. I can still hear its sound, but the roar is gentler, distant, easier.

I lie there, on this little underground beach, on my back. My fingers curl and claw the ground between me, and I find I have a fistful of small shingle. The tiny stones are perfectly smooth. They have been washed and polished by the action of the water like gemstones in a jewel polisher. Over vast periods of time they have become smooth and beautiful.

I sit up.

Rachel is standing in front of me.

"Do you know who you are?" she says, and her voice is chilling.

I shake my head, not so much at her question but more in an attempt to understand. To understand where I am, and what is happening, and why I'm still here, and why I can see in the darkness without the light of my phone ...

"Where is the boy?" I ask. "Is he here?"

"Aye," says Rachel. "He is."

"Where?" I ask, scrambling to my feet, looking around the cave. The black waters of the small lake are like a mirror, reflecting stalactites above my head so that they seem to rise upwards instead of down, from the surface of the pool.

I don't see anyone.

"Come with me," Rachel says, and wanders towards me, then past me. She takes me back to the water I have just crawled away from.

"Look!" she says, and points down at the water.

"Is he under the water?" I ask. "How? Is there another cave or ..."

"Look," says Rachel, more quietly this time, and I look.

All I see is myself, the reflection of myself, looking back up at me from the mirror-like surface of the pool.

It's then that I realise.

I turn back to Rachel, and she nods.

TWELVE

So. It's true.

In this moment, many things that did not make sense fall into place. I understand why I can see when there is no light in this cavern. I understand how I survived the journey here through the underground river. I understand why I have felt so distant from the rest of my family, why they don't answer when I speak. It makes sense now why each of them only speaks to me when no one else is around, why they don't make eye contact when they do. I know why Robbie said this is all my fault. It's to do with what happened between us this time last year, when we came to Swaledale before.

And I know who the trapped boy is. He's me.

Rachel, my great-great-great-grandmother, is looking at me. Her face is a mixture of things: concern, care, but also she wants me to understand one important thing.

"James," she says. "James, who are you?"

She starts to fade from sight.

I do not understand – I cannot answer.

I am still in shock from discovering what I am.

"No!" I cry out. "Don't leave me here! Please don't leave me trapped here!"

But Rachel is gone, leaving me alone in the cavern, which is now empty apart from the echo of her question, one last time.

Who are you?

THIRTEEN

I know now that I am a ghost. So that isn't what Rachel's question means. It has to mean something more, but I don't see what. The question repeats itself in my head, over and over.

Who are you?

Who are you?

I sit back down on the beach, and I try to work things out. I try to remember.

Bit and pieces of this puzzle fall into place like a jigsaw. I don't know what the rules are, but I know I am dead. And I know when I died.

I died a year ago, on that other Easter holiday, here in Yorkshire. Those are my last memories. My last *real* memories. In the time since then, I have not existed.

I realise now I do not remember anything after that holiday. Not school, nor home. Nothing from the entire year, not even Christmas or my birthday. Even now, on this holiday, I think I have only existed in bits and pieces. I have been bits and pieces of me, hanging around my family as they retrace their steps on this anniversary of my death. All of us have been lost in the Yorkshire landscape, all four of us ghosts in a way. And yes, they have come to scatter Granny's ashes on the hillside, but they have come to settle something with me too.

Perhaps my family's presence here has brought me back to some sort of life again, but *life* might be the wrong word, because I am dead. I am a ghost, but maybe ghosts do have life of some kind. Some kind of existence, just not one that looks like that of real, living, normal people.

I do not know the rules, if there even *are* any rules. But I think back to the few times that Robbie has spoken to me on this holiday, and now I realise he wasn't speaking to me. Not really. He was only talking because Mum believes I can hear them – that's why she keeps talking to me. That's why Dad is upset – because this stuff bothers him. That's why Robbie is angry, being forced to talk to his dead brother, being forced to talk to a ghost. He feels silly. And the only time he has spoken to me without Mum telling him to is when he's been furious, venting his anger at me. And why is he angry at me?

Because I died.

And because he feels guilty.

Because Robbie thinks it's his fault I died.

With a shock, it suddenly comes back to me. How it happened, I mean.

That scar on my knee, it's not really a scar – it's the image of what would have happened if I had survived the fall. My wound would have healed, but maybe left behind a thin white line on my skin.

I hit my head in the same moment. Without thinking, I put my hand up and rub my fingers through my hair. There, at the back of my head, slightly to one side, is the blow that killed me.

Robbie and I were playing in a river – a river that tumbled down from high on Swaledale, down waterfalls and through gullies. It's no wonder that Mum is so fearful of Robbie playing by himself now, because a year ago her two sons went out by themselves to mess around in the hillside waters, and only one of them came back.

We were jumping from rock to rock over a narrow but powerful waterfall.

I didn't want to at first, but Robbie teased me and said I was scared. I knew he was only joking, but it made me jump after him, rock to rock.

Then he slipped.

He fell into a deep pool and couldn't get out, constantly forced back under by the power of the waterfall pounding down onto him.

I didn't think. I jumped in after Robbie and fought my way towards him. Somehow, and I still don't remember how, I managed to get to him. Between us we managed to claw our way back from the downdraft of the waterfall and into the relatively calmer water again. And we thought we had made it.

We laughed. From fear and relief we laughed. Robbie said, "Bloody hell, James," just the way Dad would, and we laughed again.

All we had to do was climb out of the pool, up a short rock face beside the waterfall. Robbie went first, then turned round and leaned down, holding out his hand for me to follow.

I had my hand in his – I was that close.

But I slipped. Even as I fell and struck my knee, I thought, *That's going to hurt.* But a fraction of a fraction of a second later, my head struck a rock behind me. It knocked me out cold, and I went under the water, under the waterfall again.

I was pulled out of sight into some underground cave, which must have led to the very place I am in now. The place I am trapped.

They never found my body.

Rachel told me that I had to free the trapped boy, that only I could be the one to do it. Even as I realise that, I realise too that I am already free. All I had to do was become aware of what I am now.

In this moment, I realise that if Rachel can leave this place, then so can I. I have only been trapped by not knowing who I am – I have only been trapped because I have not seen the truth of what holds me.

Now that I do, I realise that I have power. I can leave this place at any time, and I will do so with the answer to Rachel's question. I know who I am. I am a ghost now, yes, but I *was* part of a family. It is something else I have woken up to – slowly, gradually, bit by bit. My death has fractured the family, causing it to fall apart at the seams, like an old cushion that's been kicked around like a football for years.

Dad knows it. So does Mum, in a different way. Robbie knows it, but he doesn't know that he knows it. He just knows it in a clumsy kind of way. And he doesn't want to think about it because it reminds him of how I died. Why I died, or why he *thinks* I died, at least.

I know too why my family have come back here – because my body was never found. They *know* they want to scatter Granny's ashes. But perhaps they don't realise that they are also here to look for my body. My guess is that they are pulled back here to try to find something of me, to understand what happened. To understand why I died, but there is no why. Not in my case. It was just a silly accident – it has no meaning.

And yet they are pulled here to try to make sense of the senseless, to give meaning to the meaningless. They may not know it, but I think they feel that it would bring them peace if they were to find my body. But I don't want them to see it.

I don't want them to see it, because I have just seen it myself.

I've found it. Just a few metres away from me are human remains, washed up a bit further along this strange dark shore. There is little to see. A year of decomposition has left my bones behind in rags of the clothes caught and torn on the sharper rocks higher up as I was swept down here. I recognise the jeans I was wearing that day. The T-shirt. Some hair still clings to my skull, even some skin here and there. It is a horrible sight, and I do not want them to see it, but I know I need to find a way to give my family something.

It's time to leave the cave, but I do not go alone. As I leave, I bring with me a host of other ghosts, ghosts of my family. Rachel has gone ahead, but I bring Thomas and Alfred with me. I bring their mothers and sisters and uncles and brothers.

I bring them all, for they have a story to tell. Like me, they know who they are. Part of something, something that my own family has forgotten.

FOURTEEN

I dissolve from the cave and put myself back in the open air.

It is no longer raining. A weak sun is trying to burn past a veil of cloud, cloud that is lifting and thinning. With every passing minute, the sun gets stronger and stronger.

I am at Danby High Mill, and I want to see things as they once were.

As I arrive, I see that the mill is in one piece. It has roofs, and the walls are strong and clean, not collapsing, not covered in ivy. There is life in the courtyard. A young woman walks out of one building carrying a basket of something heavy and heads towards the mill house.

She sees me, and nods and smiles, but she goes on with her business. It's like she has just seen someone she knows well, someone who lives here, someone who belongs here, both of us going about our daily work.

It is late summer – one hundred and fifty years ago. The day is hot, and the sound of the river gurgling nearby is very appealing even to me – someone who drowned in an almost ice-cold waterway.

I enter the courtyard and see three children playing with a dog, waving a stick for it to catch. The dog is leaping and barking, but in a good-natured way, enjoying this game. I pass them by and head for the mill house. It's hard to recognise as the ruin we visited on holiday. Now, as I look at it, it is a strong, powerful building. Its lines are clean and sharp. I see where the river has been diverted into a mill race – a manmade stream that enters the mill working and powers the waterwheel. This then turns the huge grindstones, milling the wheat that is brought in on carts day after day.

I duck under the low doorway of the mill house, and the noise is very great. I see the people at work inside. There are two men who look very similar in age and appearance. They could be brothers. They're organising the work of grinding the wheat, getting a team of boys and some older men to take the full sacks of flour away and stack them ready for transport.

I watch them for a while until one of the brothers notices me. He lifts a hand and smiles a gentle smile, then bends back to work.

I leave the mill house again and wander all around the buildings, smiling at everyone I see, and I wonder if they are my family. One of those boys could be Alfred, my great-great-grandfather. I don't know. It doesn't really matter, and anyway, I have to go, because there are other places to visit.

I go next to Coverham, to the sawmill.

It is one hundred and sixty years ago.

It is the same thing there. There is a beautiful and strong old building, its roof intact – under it, the place is full of life, full of work. I count sixteen people, all working, all living in this one place. They are one big family, even the one or two workers who are lodging here, lending a hand. They are not related by blood, but they live and work with my ancestors as if they are. There is no difference.

A woman comes out of the house carrying a baby. A boy. Her son. I recognise her at once. That cheeky smile, the light of her eyes. She has moved here from Crackpot Hall and fallen in love with Thomas. She is Rachel. I last saw her at the age of eight. Now she is twenty-five, and this is already her third son she is bearing, her son Alfred. My great-great grandfather. I know all this now. I know these people. I care about them.

Once more I am greeted by one or two of the family as if I belong. I wander around the sawmill because I want to see the great band saw working. Like the watermill, the saw is powered by the force of the water, turning huge cogs that send a giant, wide, flat steel saw blade humming on an endless loop, making short work of the logs that are fed to it.

It is hypnotic – not just watching the blade running but the workers tending to it, caring for it, nursing it. This blade is their work. This blade is their livelihood. This blade is their very life. Without this blade they do no work – without this blade they make no money. Without that money their lives will be over.

Suddenly, there is a tap on my back, and I turn to see I am face to face with Rachel. She's still carrying Alfred, who has gone to sleep on her shoulder.

"Isn't there something you should be doing?" she asks. There's a little dancing light playing in her eyes.

I don't know if Rachel knows who I am in this version of time. Does she remember me? Did we spend eternity together in a cave far underground, hunting secrets?

It doesn't matter. Again, it doesn't matter – what matters is that she is right. There is something I should be doing.

"Yes," I tell her, and I dissolve again and reappear at Crackpot Hall.

*

It is now.

My family are there – the current members of my family. Mum and Dad, Robbie.

They are standing in silence, each looking in a different direction. They have taken off their wet anoraks, which they have hung on a long stone wall to dry, and are feeling the warmth of the Easter sunshine on their arms.

Dad is holding the small metal pot that contained Granny's ashes. They have scattered them somewhere high on the hill and are making their way home. I'm sorry I missed the moment.

I remember Granny. She was always so kind to me. It makes me smile to think of her, and to know that she has returned home to the place from which she came, as she wanted.

Unseen, I go and sit with my family, wondering if I can talk to them, if I can communicate with them.

Dad starts talking.

"I guess I could ask at the pub. Back home, I mean," he says. "They always have people coming and going there ..."

"You're forty-five, William," Mum says to Dad. "You can't work in a pub."

"Why not?" he asks gently. "It's a job, and it's an honest job too. Pouring beer for people so they can spend their hard-earned money."

"Yes, but it's not a career, is it?"

Dad stares at Mum.

"Since when did either of us have a career? You were the closest to that for a while with your books. I can't see that we have any choice in the matter."

Mum hangs her head. She knows he's right.

Dad isn't finished.

"I worked it out," he says. "I worked out why all these big families suddenly disappear – my ancestors, I mean. You've got twenty in one place, sixteen in another. Mums and dads and grandparents and uncles and aunts, cousins and kids and then, boom! All gone. I traced the next generation or two. There's a guy living alone, working as a temporary postman in Liverpool. Another in Leeds as a handyman. A great aunt who's working as a seamstress in Manchester. They come off the land and they leave these places behind and they go to the city, and you know why?"

"Why?" asks Mum.

"The same reason I will go and ask for a job at the pub, first thing on Monday. They had to work somewhere, and the days of these old mills were over. The unstoppable tide of progress," Dad adds bitterly. "But progress for who?"

Dad waves a hand at the landscape.

"It's the same with the lead mining here too," he says to Mum. "You said it, Jane – this place is full of ghosts. As soon as there was a cheaper way of mining lead, or milling corn, or sawing planks, that was it. No more jobs on the land – people went into the city, and they did what they could. They still do."

I know he's thinking about his job. About his friends from work, also now unemployed.

I watch my family, and they are all I have. They are all *they* have. And right now, they hardly have each other. I need to do what I came to do. It is time. I need to tell them who they are. But how?

FIFTEEN

I try speaking.

It doesn't work, of course.

They can't hear me. They haven't heard anything I have said for a whole year now.

"Mum!" I cry. "Dad! Robbie?"

Nothing. I wonder if there is a trick to being a ghost – how sometimes they can be seen and heard by some people, people like Mum. But only sometimes. What makes the difference? Is it to do with the place? Or with necessity? Or with something else I haven't figured out yet?

I've only known that I am a ghost for such a short time, and suddenly it hits me. Will I live for ever now as this ghost version of me? Or will I be released from it? I feel awful, terrified, afraid. I cannot bear the thought of spending eternity alone.

But then I laugh out loud at the thought of being a ghost who's scared. It just pops into my mind what a ridiculous idea that is, and I laugh. As I do, I see Mum lift her head and turn in my direction.

"Did you hear that?" she asks.

"Hear what?" asks Dad.

Robbie just looks at her sadly.

"Never mind," she says.

I wonder at what just happened. Did Mum hear me laugh, across the border from death to life? Is it to do with laughter specifically, or is it to do with emotion in general? Is that the way ghosts speak to the living? I first heard Rachel's laugh here, but I was already a ghost then.

I go and sit next to Robbie.

He moves, ever so slightly, as I sit down next to him. I feel his sadness and guilt that have turned into anger – anger at me. Does he sense I am there? Can I make him think something? Can I make him say something?

I try. I try, I try, I try. I sit next to Robbie and I try to make him remember. I try to make him remember the day of the accident, something he spends all his time and energy trying to forget. I know it's hard for him, but I have to make him do it.

I focus on the accident. On where it happened. On where I fell. On where I ended up.

Then Robbie stirs. He scratches his head as if remembering something.

"Dad?" he says.

"Uh-huh?" says Dad.

"Did you ever figure out why this place is called Crackpot Hall when it's six miles from the village with the same name?"

Wow, I think. *My God. Have I done it?*

Dad is standing. "You know, I want to go to Crackpot," he says. "The village I mean. Anyone coming?"

Yes! I think. *That is what I need, what you need. Go to Crackpot – get in the car and go to Crackpot.*

And they do.

Of course, I am there first. They approach from the west, along the little lane that follows the south side of the River Swale, and I run across the road, right in front of the car.

Dad is driving. I don't think he sees me, but he swerves as if something has crossed their path. The car comes to a halt, its front wheels halfway up the verge.

"What?" Mum says. "What happened?"

"There was something in the road!" says Dad.

"What?" asks Robbie. "I didn't see anything."

"No, I swear I saw ..." Mum begins, but trails off.

"What?" asks Robbie again.

"No," says Mum. "Never mind. We're all OK. Just drive a little slower, will you?"

Dad starts to pull the car back off the grassy verge and is about to re-join the road. I get into the car and sit next to Robbie. I see him shiver slightly, and I know he can sense me again. I sit behind Mum. I reach out to her. I put my hands on her shoulders ...

Suddenly, Mum puts a hand on Dad's arm.

"Stop," she says.

"What?" asks Dad. "Why?"

"I ... I just ..." she says. She stops. Then she points to the side of the road. There is a small track that leads to the river. It is a beautiful warm day now, the rain long gone. It is spring. The path is inviting, and I know where it goes. I want them to take it.

"Let's just go down there," says Mum.

"Why?" asks Dad.

"That shook me – stopping like that," Mum says. "Just let me settle my nerves, please?"

Dad nods, switches the engine off.

They leave the car at the side of the lane and wander down the track that leads to the river.

I go ahead, in front of them, leading them on. I think they can all sense me now. No one is asking why they are walking to a river for no good reason. No one is arguing. They just walk as if I were really here, following me, letting me guide them. Because they need to see this space. They need to feel it.

The path opens out onto a section of the riverbank. The bank ducks right down to the water here, and there's a little beach of pebbles right beside the water, which tumbles down a low waterfall. Although it's small, it's loud, and my family will not be able to hear each other, even if they shout.

They move as if they are all dreaming, and they each come and stand with their feet in the water. It runs over the tops of their walking boots, soaking their feet in icy water. They do not seem to notice.

There are trees dotted around on the high banks of the far side. The trees cast shade down onto the river and across the waterfall, which runs fast and strong and loud. I cross the water and go and stand in its spray.

I stretch my arms out, letting the water play around my body, falling across my head, my chest. I have brought my family here. It's the closest I will ever let them get to the remains of my body that lie about twenty metres behind me, in an underground cave that no one living knows anything about.

A cave that has been long forgotten – the other end to the cave system I fell in with Rachel, the waters in which I died a year ago. A cave system that runs for six miles from Crackpot Hall to the village with the same name. A cave that people once knew about but which has been long, long forgotten. A cave which once bore the name *Raven*.

"Oh God," says Mum. "Look."

She is pointing. She cannot be heard, but she doesn't need to be heard. Dad and Robbie have seen me too – at the very least, they have seen the shape of me in the waterfall. Just a dim, flickering, splashing form, but they all know it is me. They are my family. They know me.

They stare and stare, and they move closer together, instinctively.

Eventually, I move out of the water and disappear. They step back out of the water, and then they stand in a huddle and hold each other for a long, long time.

Finally, they turn and make their way back to the car.

They do not speak.

Dad climbs into the driver's seat and starts the engine.

Mum is holding his hand. She is crying, but she is smiling. Robbie has got into the back, but just as Dad is about to pull away, his door flies open and he runs back down to the riverside.

He speaks. No one can hear his words, no living person anyway. But I do.

"James," Robbie says. "Jamie. You saved my life. But I miss you so much. So much. I love you, mate."

Then he picks up a stone and hurls it into the waterfall. I don't know if he has guessed, but the stone flies through the waterfall and into the hidden entrance to the cave. It lands just a couple of metres from the remains of what was once me.

I sit up on the high bank on the far side in the sunshine. I know I will not have to live alone for eternity now, and there is only one last thing to do.

SIXTEEN

It doesn't take very much.

That night the band are playing in the pub –
the folk band, Steel and Wool. It's the last night
of our holiday. Dad and Mum and Robbie will
leave the Yorkshire Dales and go back to our
little home. Dad will try to find work. He will
accept anything. He will have no choice. Robbie
will go back to school. Mum will go back to the
arts centre, maybe try to find something else,
full-time.

It doesn't take much of me hovering around
them to get them to stay in the pub for the
evening. They eat a nice meal, and Mum and Dad
share a bottle of wine. They even give Robbie a
little taste of it when the landlord isn't watching,
and Robbie pulls a face. Maybe he's not yet as
grown up as they all think. They listen to the
band.

The band are good. I didn't think I liked folk music, but this stuff they play is fast and lively. The songs stomp along, so that by the time night starts to fall outside, the whole pub is full of happy, smiling people – some locals, some holidaymakers, the landlord, his wife and their teenage daughter who clears tables. Watching the three musicians bring everyone together with their music.

Between songs, the lead singer and guitarist chats to the crowd. He is funny and humble, and he introduces the other two members: a woman playing the accordion and another young man playing a fiddle. It's amazing, the sound they can make with just these three instruments, and they wheel out fast song after fast song, and it's not long before people start to dance.

The night draws on, and the band are about to finish.

"I think," says the guitarist, "we will play one slow song now."

Everyone moans, but it's a friendly, jokey sound. People laugh at themselves and sit down to listen to the one slow song.

"This one is called 'The Worker'," the guitarist explains. "It goes like this."

They play the song.

People's wide smiles slowly soften into more gentle, dreamy ones.

It's a sad song, a song about working people, about how they live and how they die. How they are exploited by a tiny, tiny number of people – the rich, privileged people of the world. How this has been going on for years, decades, centuries.

As they sing and play, I watch Mum and Dad and Robbie.

Robbie moves a little closer to Dad. Dad smiles at Mum, and Mum? Mum is transfixed by the music, listening to its message: that people *are* good. In both big things and small things, most people are good. They care for each other – it's what people do, it's how they were made. You only have to look around.

Our ancestors in the mills looked after each other, worked for each other, protected each other. Mum helped that old lady who fell over in the car park. I died saving Robbie's life. I'd do it again, without thinking. It's all the same thing.

People are good, but there are a handful of people who will tell you the opposite, simply because it serves them to do so. Mostly because it helps them to get richer.

When the band finishes their song, there is a long, long silence in the pub. Not everyone gets the song. Some people think it's silly and some think it's embarrassing. But then someone starts clapping, and others join in, until maybe two thirds of the people in the pub are smiling and clapping and cheering.

"Thank you!" says the guitarist.

"No," whispers Mum. "Thank *you*."

She turns to Dad.

"Is my bag there?" Mum asks. "Beside you?"

Dad fishes for it and holds it up.

"Can I get something out for you?" he asks.

"My notebook," she says. "It's in there somewhere. Long forgotten." Mum laughs.

"Have you got an idea?" Robbie says.

"Yes," says Mum. "I think I have. I know what's been missing. I want to keep writing ghost stories. I want to write another one. But it has to mean something, do you know? It has to mean something."

Dad nods, and Robbie grins.

"Can I be in the story, Mum?" he asks.

Mum laughs.

"Sure, I'll find a role for you. For all of us."

"And Jamie too?" asks Robbie.

"Oh yes," says Mum, smiling. "He'll have the main part."

Robbie nods.

"Good," he says.

I drift away from them.

I drift away from the pub.

I lift out of the roof and up into the dark Yorkshire sky. I have remembered who I am. But in fact, I made a slight mistake. It's not that I was once part of a family. The truth is that I still *am* part of that family. I always will be. That family, *my* family, have remembered that now too. I will always be with them, even if I am dead now. Just as all our ancestors who came before me will always be a part of the huge, sprawling, branching family tree. We were there for each other. We still are.

I drift even higher.

I take one last look down at the world, and I see how beautiful it is – the lights from the pub twinkling orange into the night and the sound of one last noisy song drifting up with me into the thin cold air. The sound of people singing and laughing together. Together.

I don't need to stay any more. I'm free now.

If only it were as easy for everyone to be this free, I think.

If only.

Our books are tested
for children and young people by
children and young people.

Thanks to everyone who consulted on
a manuscript for their time and effort in
helping us to make our books better
for our readers.